Older
not wiser

Eileen Griffiths

First published as a paper back in February 2019
by Lupus Books

ISBN: 978-1-9160318-0-7

Printed and bound by CPI Group (UK) Ltd, Croydon, CR0 4YY

Design Robbie Griffiths

To my son Owen, for all the meals cooked!

Contents

As regular as Cointreau

Those squat mysterious bottles in dark coloured glass were both lifesaver and life destroyer in the summer of 1990. She'd formed another unsuitable attachment, this time with a man from Dublin working with her in London on a project. He seemed to possess the lyricism of Joyce, balanced with the rogue overtones of Brendan Behan – characteristics she considered essential in a man. She told her boss, who was doubtful. 'He's not for you,' he said. 'I've always thought of you more as a character from Yeats.' She indulged this image of herself floating whimsically in Laura Ashley dresses, but soon dismissed it, identifying more with Maud Gonne than 'Deirdre of the Sorrows'.

She knew that he'd been around a bit. He had an appealing turn to his eye giving him a 'come hither' glint, and a full moustache that drew attention to the gap in his teeth. There's a folk myth about people who have a gap between their front teeth being overly lustful, and his yawned wide. But he told her that she could be his nemesis. She knew it was a line, a good line, his trump card even, but still couldn't resist the challenge of being the one to tame him. He gave her a silver snake bracelet he'd designed that made her feel like Cleopatra; he sketched intimate portraits of her and she enjoyed being his muse; he put her on a pedestal refusing to see her feet of clay; so she allowed herself to be entranced. And that summer, despite her cautious nature, she agreed to go on holiday. It was doomed.

The big mistake was her idea to rent her cousin's apartment in Spain. This cousin was a successful businessman and she remembered him making a mad dash through Europe to buy one of these apartments when they first came on the market. She had visions of elegance, airy white rooms, a marble terrace, and an Olympic sized pool. Instead they found a 13th floor remnant from the '60s with purple walls, single camp-style beds, wonky shelves, a cracked toilet and a derisory balcony. It took them two days to find the pool, shared with another complex.

Neither of them had anticipated being thrown into such an unforgiving space with someone they scarcely knew. Awkwardness caused by lack of privacy left its legacy, permeating each day. Their relationship until then had been conducted against the backdrop of a bustling working environment and to have time stretching ahead of them, on their own, was daunting. Most days were spent on the beach, not a natural choice for her. Pale skinned she sought the shade, while he was in his element, revelling in the exposure, squatting Buddha-like in the sun. Even shopping became a bone of contention, she conceding her preference for healthier food to his more hedonistic tastes. In particular he had a voracious appetite for the cheaper cuts of red meat on which he feasted with surprising carnality; offending her fastidious soul by wiping any remains from his moustache with a flourish, finishing with a quick flick of the tongue over his upper lip. She soon came to realise that whereas the working situation had favoured the things that were common between them, this more arid environment was revealing the cracks.

Release, and there had to be some, took the form of nightly visits to 'ye olde, worlde' English pub in the basement; all you could eat and drink in '90s Spain for less than a tenner. It was a revelation to her that daylight, with its bright gaze, could be something to be avoided and this fake Dickensian lair made the perfect escape. In keeping with the '90s it offered rows and rows of fancy liqueurs. His drink was Cointreau and those promising little square bottles intrigued her. She had a problematic relationship with alcohol, knew it held danger for her, and in the past had a pattern of advancing towards it then retreating, almost daring it to capture her.

Now, in his company, she gave in without resistance, wallowing in it, allowing full saturation. And thus anointed, she emerged like Venus, reborn. She felt invulnerable, powerful, luminous and witty, aphorisms tripping from her tongue. She flowed, flirted, sparkled, and was wholly alive. This was the real love affair, not so much with alcohol as with this alcohol-created self. He was already a long established devotee of the heightened state so she joined him in the ascendancy and they revelled together, for the moment bound by their joint magnificence.

The separation began insidiously each evening. At first there was a slow ebbing away of her special powers, her protective coating dissolving, usurped by a slick of insecurity. As the evening progressed that gentle downwards slide became a speedy downhill slalom to paranoia. Those much-admired thick glass bottles now refracted and fractured the light distorting her view, and she was convinced she could see a portent of unfaithfulness in his eye as he cast a speculative glance around the bar. She imagined other women being first pierced by that wayward gaze, reeled in by his smile, getting caught in his thick moustache then being sucked in through that seemingly ever widening gap in his teeth, to be consumed.

As uncertainty tainted the atmosphere, for her, the feeling of Dickensian comfort gave way to a sense of Hogarthian unease. She tried to claw her way back to her former sense of well-being but it proved elusive. The air between them was viscous, impenetrable, and she envied the fact that he didn't seem to suffer a similar withdrawal, but remained untouched by doubt on his elevated plane. With that their final commonality was erased and as the days went by their arguments increased, punctuated by her frequent maudlin phone calls home to friends for support and validation. By the end of the week they were scarcely speaking, any connection gone, and they abandoned the apartment with great relief. They sat silently side by side on the plane on the way home, until reading about the demolition of the Berlin wall gave them scope at least for some polite conversation.

Back in London she endured her boss's 'I told you so' expression of sympathy – maybe she was less like Maud Gonne than she hoped. Luckily the project was soon over and her lover went back to Dublin leaving her space to conduct the post-mortem. She didn't so much mourn the loss of him, as her idea of him; the worst casualty being her loss of faith in her own judgement. She didn't know how to fix that though she accepted that taking alcohol out of the equation would help. That relationship had gone sour anyway. She'd embraced alcohol too recklessly, treated it with disrespect, and it had withdrawn its transient favours leaving her feeling depleted. As for love, in that area too she would gird her loins against too-easy enchantment – a neat trick if she could pull it off. But though in future she'd be wary of gap-toothed men, she suspected that she'd never entirely resist the lure of a nice turn of phrase … or someone who promised that she could be his nemesis.

Death in Venice

A litter of abandoned umbrellas told the story of the night before. It had rained continuously the previous day accompanied by strong winds, and the Turkish owner of our local supermarket, himself only recently assimilated into the idiosyncrasies of Venetian life, had taken pride in alerting us foreigners to the 'aqua alta' tide expected later that evening. We stayed safely indoors listening to the sirens sounding their warning throughout the city. The next morning we found that the tide had mostly receded leaving behind some flooded streets where trestle platforms had been erected for pedestrians.

Venice's situation is surreal anyway, having the sea continuously lapping at its houses and streets and coming up through the drains, but as we ventured out on that chilly grey November morning an extra layer of surrealism had been added. At the Biennale exhibition earlier in the week we'd observed the frequent use of discarded objects in art installations displayed in the cavernous Arsenale sheds. But that day one storm effect surpassed even those.

It seemed as though a giant hand had artfully scattered collapsed umbrellas all over Venice, huddled on humped bridges, clumped at canal sides, offering welcome splashes of colour under the lowering sky. The added height given by the walking platforms allowed us to appreciate the phenomenon even more and as we walked towards the Grand Canal we encountered a panoply of upturned umbrellas, crouched vulnerably, exposed, depleted physically and in spirit, frozen in a striking tableau, as though daylight had disturbed their nocturnal revels or maybe their mass exodus to the sea. They were dispersed singly or in strange groupings, like a pathway leading us on to some kind of umbrella limbo.

There was mass carnage near the railway station, possibly caused by people newly off trains stepping out without realising just how windy it really was. Or maybe with a surge of people cramming onto the bottleneck of a bridge where winds are trickier, eyes down to watch their step, they'd simply crashed their umbrellas into each other, the hopeless entanglement forming a twisted carapace that in foul weather no one had the patience to unmake. Was a special moment shared by those involved in this group abandonment; maybe a rueful smile? There's a certain shame in having your umbrella blow inside out, an embarrassment at a lack of handling skills, the ability to quickly adjust the angle of the umbrella to cope with shifting winds.

I'd experienced it myself the previous day when my own was wrest from my hand and borne away. I suspected that if pursued it would pause tantalisingly on its journey until I stretched out my hand to recapture it, and then some malevolence would whip it away again beyond reach. I'd known that it was foolish to put it up in such high winds in the first place but vanity, in the form of protecting newly washed hair, had prevailed. When we reached where we'd been the day before I saw a flash of a familiar purple and on getting closer realised that yes indeed, it was mine! But it now lay in a corner nestled with a sturdy gent's umbrella, looking damply at peace, and it seemed unkind to extract it from this new alliance just to dump it in a bin.

Broken umbrellas have a special pathos, like wounded birds brought down in a hurricane, as if their damaged spokes, like wings, could be re-set and they'd be ready to fly again. I imagined that this storm debris was so common in Venice that people knew to just leave their umbrellas where they lay. Surely all that metalwork and unblemished fabric couldn't go to waste and some special umbrella force trawled regularly through the city sweeping them all onto a vaporetto; spiriting them away to a secret venue to be rendered down and lovingly remade, perhaps into the ubiquitous carnival mask crowding every shop window.

We'd reached the open lagoon where the line of sky meeting sea was uninterrupted, save by the shadowy forms of the cypresses on the Isola di San Michele, the cemetery island. The day was now much brighter and in that moment of lambent light just before the sun succeeded in breaking through an opaque sky, the sea glowed and we spotted the colourful splashes of umbrellas that had escaped by being washed into the lagoon. Had they jostled with gondolas and waterbuses all the way along the Grand Canal to reach here? They'd discovered a new skill; that they could float, making use of sea breezes, fabric acting as sails, their medium still air and water; those elements no longer enemies, but now supportive friends. And they seemed to be heading in that direction, like miniature boats of Charon, to the island of the dead.

Conditional love

They were in one of those beach cafes that extended breakfast service to midday, to cater for surfers maybe. One of those cafes with bleached wood tables painted sea green outside, and shells and pieces of driftwood tastefully displayed inside. It was too early in the season for surfers and the café had its share of middle-aged tourists like themselves and a phalanx of local mothers and babies. It boasted of its homemade food and her mushroom on toast came with a white bean 'favette' and mushroom tapenade on the side. Surfers must be discerning eaters. It was delicious.

'I'm glad that you eat nicely,' he said. She suspended operations and looked up warily. Was this a sarcastic comment on the fact that she didn't use a knife or on the frenzy with which she was despatching her food? But no, he was sincere.

'I wouldn't find you as endearing if you didn't have good table manners, if you were a messy eater or spoke with your mouth full.'

He'd made similar remarks before and although so far she'd always been on the right side of the judgement the very idea of being judged rankled a bit. At the concert yesterday he'd praised her outfit but had been critical of some hapless woman who'd seemingly got it wrong, making her wonder if all the times he didn't comment he was secretly disapproving. But it was early in their relationship, and up to now she'd chosen just to accept the remarks as the compliments she supposed they were. Today, maybe something about the comfortable atmosphere of the place and the mainly female clientele, gave her courage to risk pulling the whole thing down around their ears and to take a stand.

'When you say things like that it sounds as though you've appointed yourself as the grand arbitrar of what's acceptable. I feel as though I'm being continuously interviewed for a job and you're telling me that I'm doing all right so far!' He had the grace to bow his head in recognition.

'So it's not unconditional love then?' she teased, to take the heat out of her comment.

She actually felt pretty secure in his love, he told her all the time didn't he, said there wasn't anything he disliked about her though she suspected she was about to introduce a few. He always said that he valued her openness, as well he might given that she'd only been complimentary about him so far. She doubted that he could take the rough with the smooth.

'There's no such thing as unconditional love,' he proclaimed, 'we live in the real world. Everyone must have some criteria of behaviour that's unacceptable to them.'

She knew that this was true, pondering her own deal breakers, one of which this characteristic of his might prove to be further down the line. Or she would ultimately come to grief, shipwrecked on one of his.

They finished eating and as they left the café she noticed a smear of egg at the side of his mouth. She didn't just intimately wipe it off as she may have done the day before, but pointed it out to him, innocently and without emphasis, certain, after what he'd said, that the significance wouldn't be lost on him. As she preceded him out the door she allowed herself a wry smile, accompanied by a triumphantly sibilant, 'YES!'

Ben

She hasn't spoken to him in 15 years, doesn't know if he's dead, doesn't want to know, prefers to think of him now as he was then, the most thrillingly alive person she's ever known. He was her best friend and she his muse for twenty years, lovers for a very short time towards the end which she viewed merely as a postscript to their story, a brief consummation, something that added an extra flavour to later memories. Her affair with alcohol was initiated, tended and progressed congruently with their friendship, so closely entwined that she often wondered if either could have stood alone or been so rich in texture. He was her Sancho Panza, riding shotgun on her adventures, bearing witness to her life.

His face
rises to the surface,
shifting aside those who came after.

She caught Kurt Vonnegurt's devil-may-care laugh on the radio the other day and was right back there in some bar, curled up beside Ben, he gesturing with his cigarette as he threw back his head and laughed, the laughter coinciding with the blowing out of smoke. She could hardly remember a time when the two didn't go together, letting the laughter and smoke expel anything righteous or ridiculous.

His lovely insouciant laugh
ascending,
buoyed up by snakes of smoke.

Like quicksilver, so hard to pin down, simultaneously so exposed and so hidden that she once described him who was so alive, incongruously, as a parody of himself. He laughed and took it as his due, yet there was intransigence at his core. People who'd moved out of his life were dead to him he said, forgotten, though she couldn't quite believe that, was sure it couldn't happen to her. Still, his animated face is fixed as clearly as when they first met, indelibly imprinted on her mind, as though the top layer of molecules of her being had undergone an irreversible reaction with his, had fused to form an unfissionable bond.

His image
as sharp as an engraving,
etched into her psyche.

Of course it was love, of a kind, she has his letters still, and when she reads them his voice speaks out to her with all the immediacy and dear familiarity of the past. Those long erudite letters bubbling with humour, love only mentioned obliquely in convoluted sentences that had to be read a number of times to get the meaning, but nonetheless permeating every line. Letters that gave gracious advice on all her relationships yet never really considered anyone good enough for her, letters so full of faith in her uniqueness and ability to conquer that they're still a source of comfort to her even now. He took her pale offerings, spun them into gold and reflected back to her a more vital, radiant version of herself. She recalled that line, full of yearning, in a poem by Yeats, 'But one man loved the pilgrim soul in you' ... and knew he was that one.

To be worthy
of that love,
its distilled essence lingering.

Schrodinger's Cat

Schrodinger's cat lies curled in the box, half dead, half alive, literally. Well maybe not literally, but conceptually, because she's been placed there in order to demonstrate a concept in quantum physics. Her relationship with the scientist Schrodinger is purely cursory – he got her from the cat pound for the purpose of this experiment. He never inquired about her name or attempted to name her himself; her designation in the experiment's title is merely as his possession. In fact her name is Tiddles and she takes pleasure in the incongruity of this in connection with such a highfalutin' experiment.

According to quantum theory she's simultaneously dead *and* alive in the box until it's opened and the observation of her *causes* her to be either dead *or* alive. When she's observed to be either dead or alive then a whole history comes into being, backwards in time, as to how she got to this state. Tiddles is rather annoyed about this – she knows her own back history thank you very much, she doesn't want some bloke called Schrodinger having the power to rewrite it for her. More importantly, she doesn't relish the idea of her possible death. Because her box also includes a Geiger counter that will 'fire' if an atom enters the box, resulting in a lever pulling a cork from a bottle of hydrogen cyanide. Tiddles is only too aware that hydrogen cyanide is poisonous, and that whether or not it's released is a random event. Schrodinger is playing Russian roulette with her life.

One thing she has got in common with him is that they both think that quantum physics says something 'absurd'. Tiddles has heard that it's all about the possibility of an atom being in two places at the same time, parallel universes and that kind of stuff. She's learnt that quantum physics is problematic when you try to extrapolate the behaviour of micro atomic particles and relate it to the 'real' macro world of things like tables and chairs. Tiddles knows that she lies somewhere along the spectrum between micro and macro and that's why she's been chosen. She ruminates on the sorry position in which she now finds herself. It's said that only when pets are pampered like babies can you say that a country has developmentally and economically arrived. For example North Korea has seemingly now 'arrived'. Tiddles in the past has herself enjoyed such lavish treatment before unfortunately landing up in the cat pound. But no such consideration is being accorded to her in this particular experiment, taking place in a supposedly sophisticated environment. She's the sacrificial cat, with even odds on her survival.

But Tiddles is determined not to die; she's nearing the end of her nine lives and doesn't want to throw another one away needlessly. She has a trick up her furry sleeve. She has found it hard to escape from the constant droning on of the scientists in Schrodinger's team and is now using it to her advantage. One of the pieces of information she's absorbed is Heisenberg's 'Uncertainty principle', which states that the very observation of a particle can cause it to change its position. In fact if she survives she's thinking of amalgamating the two concepts 'Schrodinger's cat' and the 'Uncertainty principle' and inventing her own theory called 'Tiddles – the Uncertainty Cat'. Because she knows that her actions could add a new layer of physical uncertainty to the experiment; rewrite the equation even.

While lying there Tiddles has been thinking outside of the box. Her coup de grâce is that she's an aware, cognizant creature. She has figured out that if Schrodinger is an observer, then though a mere cat so also is she, and that she can use Heisenberg's principle to influence any atom that might infiltrate the box. If there's one thing cats do particularly well it's to stare. She's pretty confident that by observing the offending particle and fixing it fiercely in her gaze, she can unnerve it enough to deflect it from setting off that Geiger counter and releasing the gas. In her isolation she's keeping herself buoyant by imagining the look on their faces as they open the box and she explodes out claws exposed – it's no less than they deserve. Time may be relative but she feels like she's been in the box for eons. She hopes that Schrodinger has had the foresight, given the chance of her survival, to have at least bought some cat food. Tiddles knows that she might be a conceptual cat, even a virtual cat, but she doesn't care. Tiddles is very hungry.

Afterwards

Looking back, she couldn't quite pinpoint the time when the exchange of air between them had become unequal. The portrait of her hanging over the marble mantelpiece, painted shortly after they'd first moved in, showed her as statuesque and proud with her arm resting proprietarily on that same mantel. She seemed to occupy her space with ease then, to stand her ground, though maybe there was a hint of strain around those eyes even then.

It was a grand house and over the years she felt that as he had grown in stature to fill it, she had diminished accordingly. As though he was sucking in her air, inhaling her exhaled breath and channelling it somehow to nourish and sustain his own well-being. She sought and found the reflection of her slight figure in the milky depths of the mirror on the wall facing her, and feared that the process was now irrevocably complete.

Sitting upright, still in her dark clothes, her pale starkness was emphasised against the sofa's bright green brocade. The tea tray in front of her was a reminder that others would be arriving soon to offer comfort, but she was frozen in place, immensely grateful for this interlude of quiet. She breathed in and exhaled, was surprised that this time her breath hovered, remained hers.

Although it had a fine Georgian window, this was always a room where the focus was inwards. He'd liked to have the blinds down to deter the sunlight from his desk and in any case there was nothing to encourage the gaze outwards as the

15

view of the imposing houses opposite did little to relieve her spirit. This room was all about the internal, and an observer looking in would have judged it a picture of framed perfection. She was aware that she existed in a lavish 'still life', which she'd allowed to stultify and still her own life.

It was filled with items collected by both of them over the years, but whereas he'd still had the lust for accumulation she had reached saturation point many years ago. At some point it had ceased to be a pleasure for her, maybe when she realised that the objects now belonged here while she no longer did. The room weighed heavily on her, everything in it competing for space, clamouring for attention. Her eyes were weary as they drifted over the pieces trying to absorb their rich detail, their beauty only making them more deadly, flaunting their permanence in the face of an impermanent life.

It came to her that she could now pare everything down to the bone, though she felt sad when she considered what lives are reduced to when reviewed through the things left behind. The distilled essence of all their early hopes and dreams still lingered in these objects and it seemed disloyal to now have solitary control. She wondered how much time would have to pass before they lost their potency and could be respectfully abandoned.

She took a breath and it felt pure, nourishing, fanning those embers still glowing within her. She heard a knock and took another deep life-stirring breath. She prepared herself. They had arrived.

Flights of Fancy

We struck it lucky, Edie and I, on the second night of our stay in that small Italian town, coming upon a full dance band playing waltzes in the square. And what a square! It was surrounded by grand old gothic buildings propped up by well-established palm trees that looked slightly incongruous in that place of faded formality. This was a prosperous spa town where the conservatively well-to-do, rather than the flamboyantly rich, flocked annually on pilgrimage to sample the waters. Definitely old money rather than new. Around the edges of the square were cloisters. Now, I'm a sucker for cloisters. I think that some image must once have been imprinted on my young subconscious, of a sunlit garden surrounded by pale green shading arches. I suspect it was from a religious painting where an archangel hovered waiting to deliver a miraculous message to an unsuspecting virgin; but I've spent my life trying to rediscover that oasis of calm and well-being.

This place wasn't it, but it had enough points of comparison to add an extra frisson of magic to the occasion. These cloisters were definitely secular in nature, being indented with posh cafes selling overpriced architectural cup cakes, alternating with tasteful leather-ware boutiques. Mature couples, urbane and well preserved, occupied the tables around the band. Edie and I had made an effort to dress for the evening, but in comparison to them I felt like an island of awkwardness in a sea of effortless elegance. The women nonchalantly shrugged off their fur coats and left their designer handbags unattended as they got up to dance. Our provincial reaction to this act of seeming madness was to appoint ourselves as informal guardians of the neighbouring tables, but we became aware that our services were unnecessary.

A sudden breath of wind set the fur rippling as though muscles long dormant were shaking off their lethargy and flexing in anticipation of renewed action. Given form by the chairs on which they'd been so casually draped, the countless small mammals woven together in these fur coats miraculously combined spirits to re-animate and assume the characteristics of much larger beasts, eager to rear up and escape their confines. These age-old symbols of the bourgeoisie were ready to perform their class function and envelope, claw and crush any marauding masses, leaving their owners free to dance sedately, seemingly unaware, no blood on their innocent hands. The designer handbags with their fierce metal clasps ready to snap off any errant fingers were a second line of defence.

Then an elderly gentleman approached our table and asked Edie to dance. She, overcome by the occasion, demurred and he turned to me, my enthusiasm overcoming any feelings of inadequacy. Looking very dapper in a dinner jacket and highly polished brogues, he radiated such vitality that I could almost see the mineral spa water effervescing through his frame. But so tiny that I worried I'd overpower him when I stood up. Possibly I imagined the clicking of his heels as he formally held out his hand, but when I arose to take it, he seemed taller. And maybe it was because the music changed just then but I like to think that he detected in me a budding Ginger Rogers, because he whirled us off to the edge of the square and around those cloisters in the style incarnated by her and Fred in their iconic movies.

The energy pulsing through his body passed to me through his touch, like an electrical discharge. He generously allowed me to be the one to rise to the occasion, the one to take flight.

I was suddenly weightless, floating, soaring and spinning as though suspended on celestial wires – the woman in a painting by Chagall; the closest I've come to frictionless motion, a state I've always yearned for; my only connection to the ground being my tenuous hold on my dinner-jacketed partner who gazed up with pride, amazed at my skill. He didn't take any credit for my performance other than that of someone who'd serendipitously chosen the perfect partner. Then the music came to an end, gravity re-imposed its pull and I floated down to take my place by his side. He bowed and led me back to my table, dizzy, drained. As I sat down the connection was finally broken, and I was left feeling an outsider again.

Grateful though I was for his brief moment of support, I was resentful of being dependent on someone like him for my energy, my buoyancy, my uplifting, and my rare sense of belonging. I resolved next day to drink my full share of that same spa water, that fountain of life that gave my octogenarian soul mate his valiant vigour; to immerse myself in that bountiful elixir and benefit from the alchemical process that would turn me from 'other' to 'accepted'; to imbibe, as I hadn't with my mother's milk, that elusive air of insouciance, power and privilege; ultimately to become one of them.

The Moment

It's not the kind of room for bad news. Limpid light filters through latticed screens; a tree on the veranda, heavy with white blossom, is reflected in a wall mirror that brings even more light into the room. The two sisters are draped in rich Vermeer type fabrics, the youngest sitting on a broad low stool, the elder uncharacteristically ensconced at her feet cocooned in a voluminous rug.

In their parents' absence they'd opened the letter from a family friend, the younger reading the news first, slightly puzzling over the vernacular from a neighbouring province while her elder sister languidly interprets it later as the hand scroll unfurls down towards her. The younger sister relishes the novelty of the situation, its first hand quality. She's used to receiving everything at second hand, life, experiences, and now love. Because she loves her sister's betrothed, her sister older than her by less than a year and, as is customary, having her marriage arranged first.

She'd fallen in love at one remove through paper thin walls as formal introductions took place in another room, between the two sets of parents, the young man and her sister, everything she learned filtered through them. On the first occasion that she, the younger sister, had been introduced directly to him, she'd felt a quickening of the spirit and imagined she'd caught some reflection of her own excitement in his face. On subsequent occasions she'd caught his covert looks of interest and telegraphed a chaste response from hooded eyes.

And now, months later she progressed through this innocuous letter, full of ritual greetings and trivialities, family news. Then the tone seemed to change and embedded in the next line was a small silent nugget of destruction. Their friends sought to inform them of a death, the suicide of a young man of their acquaintance. Her sister's betrothed and her unacknowledged lover. Now anguish battles in her emotions with an insidious voluptuous kind of pride. If she was ever in doubt of his love, his taking the only honourable way out of the dilemma confirms it. This was his first and final message directly to her and by some serendipitous twist of fate she had actually received it first. For one terrible, glorious moment she hugs this news to herself, claims this death for herself, holds it like a guilty secret for her eyes only. This is her validation, her grief-tainted triumph.

Then she remembers her sister, physically and metaphorically at her feet, for a short time in her power. Should she warn her? Surely it isn't the younger sister's duty to protect and comfort. Her Noh-like face masking the cataclysmic end, she watches her sister with an unashamed voyeur's anticipation. This time her reactions would be the original, merely mirrored by an older sister receiving second hand news, experiencing tragedy at second hand. But as she waits poised for her response, she has an intimation of the future, is struck by the realisation that her sister would still claim the ultimate revenge as the one to be pitied, to be consoled, while for her a life of unacknowledged grief beckons.

Younger by less than a year – such a minor detail to dictate fates and have the power to devastate. Not a room for bad news, but as a cloud passes and the light dims she watches her sister's face begin to crumple.

Culture Vulture

I used to be precious about old stones, obsessed with them, I was a stone junkie: stones in the form of historical buildings, statues, ancient ruins, or the odd balcony in Verona. I was always the tourist with my nose in the guidebook, keeping my finger on my place on the page so I could resume as quickly as possible as I tracked down all of the 3-star rated attractions, most of the 2-star, and as many of the 1-star as I could cram in. I was a culture voyeur – other people's reactions were almost more important than my own. I would escort friends around new places not allowing them to deviate from the recommended route. I would guide them to a magnificent building or piazza metaphorically blindfolding them by taking them via dark side streets, and when we finally emerged into the light I'd go 'ta-dah!' and wait for their reactions.

I was invariably disappointed. My friend Valerie, for example, would oblige for about thirty seconds, say 'that's amazing' and then her gaze would slide down the building to the shops round the edge of the square leaving me feeling strangely unfulfilled. Even when I took her to the Sistine Chapel, after looking up for a good few minutes she got restless as if to say … what, no shops? I admit I was a stone snob. I was shocked when I took my aunt to the medieval walled city of Lucca and she said, 'It could do with a lick of paint.' She would scan the buildings for that little piece of stonework that had been restored, and say 'that's nice and clean, it'll be great when it's all finished.' I was disdainful of people who said they didn't do sightseeing on holiday anymore – they just relaxed. Relaxed!

I couldn't sit in a café or on a beach for more than an hour without dashing off to see that little building round the corner so I could tick it off my list.

Then things gradually changed. After a number of holidays with Valerie she eventually won me over, I was infected, seduced by the siren call of leather goods and jewellery, and went to the dark side. I like to think that it was due to my anti-commercialism principles that I hadn't indulged in such pursuits before, but the truth is that there was part of me thought that I was above things like shoe shops. Maybe it was just that shoes had rejected me, because with flat feet and bunions my choices were always going to be less glamorous than Valerie's. Cruising shops for that special little 'comfortable' shoe just isn't as much fun! As for jewellery, I was proud of my more ethnic, philistine taste, so buying my first gold piece was like being a kid in a sweet shop. Once I was on the slippery slope there followed holidays where we scoured shops and remote designer outlets for that perfect 'thing'. I was by then on a downhill shopping slalom culminating on the shameful day I actually bought co-ordinating handbag and shoes! I never wore them together, but that's not the point, enough was enough. Luckily it all petered out quite naturally. For various reasons Valerie and I didn't travel together for a while and then I found myself pretty much reverting to my former 'stony' self.

But I knew that I couldn't go back there. When I thought seriously about my early behaviour, one incident stood out. I was having dinner with some friends in what was once a 12th century palace. They got a bit boisterous and I was trying to shush and silence them because they weren't showing enough reverence. In retrospect I realised that what I was doing was sterile. Life is for living and all they were doing was creating new memories within the old. After all, these old places were themselves just the stage setting against which other people once played out real, ordinary lives. By paying such homage, I was letting the stones and their stories weigh me down and stifle and suppress the creation of my own.

So my best memories of Valerie aren't the statues or buildings we saw together, but us spending a weekend in Barcelona in the summer heat shopping for winter boots. And her always saying, whatever impossible shoes she tried on, that they were 'really comfortable, they fit me like a glove' (even our analogies were accessory based), then being in agony before we got to the end of the street! I suppose I did get a little bit of flat-footed revenge after all.

I'm not saying that life is too short for old stones, but I'm putting those stones back in their proper, rightful place. Compromise is everything. I can appreciate and respect them while letting their stories inform and enhance my own experiences, which will be just as valid.

And I am weaning myself off my stone frenzy, honest. But sometimes I have withdrawal symptoms and relapse. For example, I was the only one who on a recent tour, ran all the way to the end of the promontory to see the Roman Grotto of Catullus in 35°C, while everyone else just ate ice cream in the square. I once heard it said that 'the presence of tranquillity in a work of art speaks of a great internal civilisation'. I was admiring the art of great civilisations without somehow embracing that tranquillity and letting it be reflected in myself. And then I recently read a quote in an old church that also struck a chord. It said 'the days spent in these ancient places give us a time of serenity, to better grasp the beauty and meaning of things, to enable us to rediscover the deep and solid roots of life, so that we can give flavour to every moment, every activity and every human relation.' I liked that. And that's just what I'm going to do next time. I promise!

The Alternative Creation

It was the evening of the sixth day, and land, sky, sea, light, all were in place. She was exhausted but proud of what she'd created – although there'd been the issue with the humans. The original concept had been sound enough, the universe was based on the physical laws of opposites attracting, so why not apply it to humans? And it would be so much easier wouldn't it, to start with two and let them reproduce, than to have all the hassle involved in instant mass population? So she'd created male and female, and that's when the trouble started.

Maybe the mistake had been to create the male first and the female from one of his spare parts. This seemed to have endowed him with a sense of superiority over the female, who coming second, became a natural handmaiden. Even the names they instantly chose for themselves reflected this. For the male, Adam, said with a bit of swagger, sounding so much like '*I* am' (ever wonder where the word adamant meaning 'I'm right and you'd better believe it' comes from?). And for the female, gentle Eve, short for (eve)r ready to please. She replayed the scene in her mind – Adam reclining languidly in the Garden of Eden while he sent Eve off to forage for food. She'd been so anxious to prove that she could take the initiative that she'd succumbed to the salesman patter of the sleazy snake-in-the-grass, and plucked the apple. So contrary to popular myth, Eve was the temp***ted*** not the temp***tress,*** and she didn't have to do the dance of the seven fig leaves to entice Adam to bite. Oh no, he, thinking that nothing should be denied to a man of his excellent birthright, took little persuasion in accepting the proffered fruit.

She sighed – she could see this pattern of inequality repeating itself for what seemed like an eternity. But it would be too much effort to start over again. Maybe if she could make some small technical adjustment, just to redress the balance of what she now saw as a basic design fault? 'Got it,' she thought and metaphorically snapped her fingers. Adam awoke with a brief sense of well-being and then shot up with an agonised look, hands cradling his much swollen stomach. 'Do I look bloated to you?' he asked, and as Eve tried to reassure him, threw himself to the ground, his cry of 'It isn't fair,' echoing to the heavens!

Goddess permitted herself a gentle smirk. She had to admit, that move had been a stroke of genius. Being potentially out of action for nine months every few years would certainly 'cramp' Adam's style. Well, if she didn't have the divine right to pun who did? She was sorely tempted to leave things but no, she'd had her fun, how on earth would he cope? Reluctantly she snapped her fingers again and Adam reawakened. 'I've had the strangest dream,' he muttered to Eve, shrugging off the unwelcome memory. After he'd surreptitiously checked out his restored six-pack he relaxed once more into his earlier state of languor and entitlement and directed Eve, 'Fetch me another one of those apples, dear!'

Goddess tuned out, wearily. Land, sky, sea, light ... and humans. A flawed masterpiece, but she'd done her best. Let them get on with it. Tomorrow was a day of rest, she'd chill out, listen to the celestial choir, maybe turn some water into wine ... a woman's work was never done.

Cut and Thrust

-- *'How was the lunch the day after the wedding?'*
-- *'Actually there was a bit of a strange atmosphere, the bride...'*
-- *'Who was there?'*
-- *'All her side of the family...'*
-- *'And his side?'*
-- *'His mother and sister, but as I was saying...'*
-- *'Were they hung over then?'*

When challenged he calls this twenty questions approach his contribution to the conversation. She calls it extremely frustrating. 'It's just part of the normal to and fro,' he says, but she feels there's a lot more to-ing than fro-ing. They're still only in the foothills of the interruption stakes here, the giving him the benefit of the doubt stage, where he acts like a giant over-enthusiastic puppy dog waiting for a conversational stick to be thrown so that he can chase it down, worry it for a while and present it back to her, tail wagging wildly.

-- *'Carol and I want to walk the Camino later this year if...'*
-- *'Oh yes! I did that two years ago, well the last 110 kilometers so that I could get the certificate.'*
-- *'if Carol's knee gets a bit better, otherwise...'*
-- *'My knee was giving me problems too towards the end, but overall it was very satisfying to know that I could accomplish it.'*
-- *'otherwise we'll have to go on one of those tours where they carry your luggage...'*
-- *'Oh yeah ... yeah ... I know ... yeah.'*

This is a more competitive mode, where he reminds her of a basketball player marking an opponent, mirroring her every move, ready to snatch at any conversational ball that strays his way. Those 'yeahs' are like the relentless bounce of that ball being dribbled tantalisingly in front of her face. They should be reassuring, evidence that he's listening at least, but instead they're an annoying voiceover, each word a sharp punctuation that scrapes at her nerves, a reminder that the conversation is only on short term loan and would soon be back with its rightful owner.

-- *'Monica was a bit subdued when I met her today. She hasn't been feeling well recently, she's waiting for the results of a thyroid test...'*
-- *'I've never needed to have one of those so I don't know what they might show, but...'*

Really? Was he really hijacking this conversation just to tell her what he didn't know? Was what he didn't know so much more valuable than what she might? If queried he would say that he was encouraging her, that he loved the sound of her voice and hated his own so she wondered why he was so intent on silencing her. She had broached this subject when their love was new and she was naïve enough to think that a few playful remarks would do the trick but he didn't see that he was doing anything wrong; no one had ever had a problem with him before.

She accepted that her own speech patterns were less linear than his, more circuitous. She imagined her own telling of a story as akin to weaving a tapestry where you have to wait patiently for the overall pattern to emerge. It was true that sometimes she lost the main thread and the telling edged dangerously close to Yeats's 'widening gyre' where the centre cannot hold. Maybe she should school herself to wait until she had her argument neatly corralled and trimmed around the edges before spitting it out in the manner of players on the radio programme 'Just a Minute', without hesitation or deviation, allowing no chinks where wedges could be driven in.

-- *'I want you to listen to me without saying anything until I'm finished.'*
-- *'Nothing at all?'*
-- *'Nothing.'*
-- *'Okay.'*

He seemed to respect this approach, maybe saw it as a bit of a game; but this technique was more suited to important subjects, she surely couldn't preface every sentence with this? Or they could adopt a conversational codeword like that used to break an S&M session, to show your partner that he's crossed a line and you're not willing to play anymore. She found that as a last resort using an extended silence to indicate her annoyance worked to an extent, he did eventually notice, but it felt too much like capitulation on her part, a kind of own goal.

-- *'They were obviously hung over the morning after the wedding but it was more than that...'*
-- *'When are they going on their honeymoon?'*
-- *'Not for a few days and maybe that was the problem, it meant there was an awkward break in the romantic flow that allowed reality to seep in...'*
-- *'Where are they going?'*
-- *'Sicily... but they had come down to earth with a dull thud, everyone deflated and morose. If they...'*
-- *'I love Sicily.'*
-- *'For God's sake let me finish!'*
-- *'Go ahead!'*
-- *'If they survive that they'll survive anything!'*

Sins of the Mother

Jane woke to the sound of sobbing downstairs, disturbing the early morning quiet. The sound was further unexpected because she could tell it came from an adult, and after a few minutes she realised it was her mother's sister, Margaret. They lived in adjoining terrace houses, Jane's family in one and her grandfather and an assortment of aunts and uncles, including Margaret, in the other. This closeness encouraged, if not enforced them, to live in an expansive extended family kind of way. There were nine siblings in her mother's family and next door acted as a hub for all social occasions.

Despite her father's alcoholism, and the absence of any affluence, Jane had always felt that her childhood was fairly idyllic; but like every family, fault lines ran beneath the surface. Aunt Margaret had had an illegitimate daughter, Rita, which was wildly problematic in their community at that time. Even Margaret's brother and sister, who lived with her, said that they felt the disgrace, so Rita had been despatched to live with a great aunt and uncle in a small rural village about thirty miles away. Although it was never discussed, Jane vaguely knew of the situation, and her main contact with Rita, a few years older than Jane, was when she, her brothers and a full complement of cousins, were packed off each summer to equally enjoy or suffer the exotic attractions of country life. While the adult supervision varied from the laid-back to the criminally lax, the children formed gangs based on the hierarchical principles of age and gender and terrorised the countryside.

Maybe this was where the seeds of Rita's subsequent rebellion were sown, but Jane envied Rita's freedom to come and go as she pleased; one of her best memories being of Rita leading her in a precarious climb onto the roof of the cottage at 6 am one morning, to admire the 'manly structure' of a farmer's son working in a field nearby. When she reached the age of thirteen and was undisputedly beyond the great aunt's power of control, Rita returned to school in town, and to the house next door. By then the objecting aunt and uncle had emigrated to sunnier climes. The few years age difference between Jane and Rita now assumed greater significance and Jane had had less contact with her older cousin in the last few years.

That Saturday morning, concerned at her aunt's cries, Jane crept downstairs to where her mother was comforting her sister, 'I'm sure she'll come back soon and things will get sorted out.' Aunt Margaret remained unconsoled, but looking up caught sight of Jane lingering tentatively in the doorway. 'We might as well tell her,' Margaret said, 'she'll know soon enough anyway.' Jane's mother was reluctant, her natural tendency being to filter reality of its more uncomfortable aspects before disseminating it. She also felt a fleeting resentment at the fallout this incident would have on her own family. Nevertheless she agreed, and Jane learnt that Rita had absconded to England overnight with her slightly older boyfriend. She knew that Aunt Margaret didn't approve of this boyfriend, whom she considered feckless because he preferred to occupy himself playing his guitar rather than getting a 'proper job'. In her innocence Jane didn't think this sounded too bad – in fact she had a sneaking admiration for her suddenly grown up cousin.

Then they dropped the bombshell and Jane discovered the true cause of her aunt's anguish – Rita was pregnant. She'd explained everything in a note Margaret had found on the kitchen table that morning – she intended to have the baby and set up a new life with her boyfriend in London. The note was devoid of details or any logistics; instead it made everything sound simple, not deserving of fuss. But for Margaret of course the event was of huge significance. Seventeen years ago she'd found herself in the same situation and despite all efforts at education and indoctrination to ensure that Rita would never suffer the same fate, history had repeated itself. Almost as though her constant warnings had, by some terrible irony, imprinted and attracted the feared outcome rather than prevented it. Was this the ultimate divine retribution, the sins of the mother being visited on her child?

Jane's mother had a moment of doubt, wondering whether her own constant cautioning of her children against the evils of alcohol would have a similar effect, and by some perverse law of nature they'd end up following in their father's footsteps. But as for Jane, at fourteen, she just felt the edge of something slightly dangerous insinuating itself into her life, that threatened to squeeze out the remains of childhood and project her into an uncertain future.

Winners and Losers

That July afternoon the four women set out on a treasure hunt that had been designed by the lover of one of them. Members of a drama group, they were on the third day of their annual pilgrimage to a small town in Galway to perform with their sister group who were based there. It was customary for the Belfast group to perform a Yeats play, dark and redolent with angst, complemented by a frothier concoction from their Galway counterparts. This Galway drama group was composed of the town's luminaries, the doctor, bank manager, candlestick maker etc. The lover was the local dentist, like them in his 50s, married of course, a heavy drinker but in true Behan tradition, endlessly witty.

The other three women had been making this journey for many years and were used to the lover situation but Jenny, relatively new to the group, was not. When Diana had mysteriously disappeared from rehearsals the previous day, the others considered it expedient to let her in on the secret. Jenny knew that Diana was in a relationship back home and was surprised that she would risk it in this way. She may also have felt some moral ambivalence about the situation, but Diana assured her that she and her lover met only a few times a year and that the arrangement was mutually life enhancing. Besides Jenny hadn't met his wife yet. In truth she was maybe a little envious. She'd had a lengthy conversation with the lover the previous evening when he was on the upward slopes of inebriation and found him charming. Furthermore, she didn't think that Diana had the same capacity as herself to really appreciate his humour and she also felt that this kind of long distance relationship, infrequent but with maximum excitement, would exactly suit her own temperament.

They're in Colette's car, Diana in the passenger seat and Carol and Jenny squashed in the back. Colette plays the cello for a living travelling from wedding to funeral, her small car a mobile home crammed with the instrument itself, various changes of clothing, bags of accessories and all the accoutrements for dining on the road if necessary. Jenny shifts uncomfortably in the back, jostling for space with the neck of the cello case and various stage props, but she stoically accepts this as a reflection of her position as newcomer in the group.

Their destination is the Burren, an area of great geographical interest, and they navigate the country roads as instructed by the lover, until after an hour they're satisfied that they've arrived at exactly the right spot. They climb out of the car with relief. 'We're to look for a white-splashed rock with a red marker of some kind,' reads Diana with excitement, and in the spirit of her huntress namesake leads them over the low wall. They gaze in awe at the endless expanse of barren limestone. 'It looks like the birds have stained all the rocks with white!' Colette remarks, with some misgiving. There are no obvious red markings either but still they fan out and begin the search with enthusiasm. They concentrate first on the immediate area, Diana nimbly leaping from rock to rock innately guided by love. The others, not so favourably supported, pick their way more gingerly, allowing mundane thoughts of broken limbs and the doubtful logistics of rescue in such an isolated place, to slow them down.

After thirty minutes of anticipatory search, enthusiasm is definitely waning and Diana admits, 'It's not here, we'll have to spread further apart.' They head off in diverse directions drifting raggedly, until all semblance of rational process is abandoned. 'Surely he wouldn't have made it this difficult?' Carol thinks. She's distracted; she's always loved the Burren, its spiritual quality instilling in her a deep-seated serenity. Today doesn't disappoint, everything is bathed in a pellucid light and she yearns to just wander off on her own, giving in to the visceral pull of the horizon and embracing the drama of the deep rock fissures. Diana on the other hand is anxious, knowing that the search is becoming hopeless but not wanting to give up. 'Where could it possibly be?' she cries out in frustration. The others, hearing her, are aware that she's on the verge of tears and steel themselves for a renewed effort to make the rocks yield up their treasure.

After another tense fifteen minutes Jenny suddenly shouts, 'Over here, I think I see something red!' They scramble over trying not to build up their hopes, but there indeed is a red balloon, obviously the intended marker, which has deflated and collapsed into the cleft. Attached to it is a package. 'Let me get it,' says Diana, pushing past Jenny. She forages around in the hole and emerges triumphantly brandishing a bottle of champagne with a card in a plastic sheath. The others are pleased for her and for themselves. 'I knew it,' she says in vindication of the lover, 'we've searched thousands of square yards but here it was after all, only ten yards from the road!' Once back at the car Colette produces four glasses from somewhere, not quite champagne flutes but good enough, and they toast the absent lover. Diana's tears are in full flow now as she reads the card, 'He hopes that we all enjoy the champagne...' and then as she reads greedily ahead, stops. 'The rest is definitely for my eyes only,' she says, her giggles supplanting tears.

Buoyant with communal good feeling and not a little tipsy, they all pile back into the car, which now magically appears more accommodating. About a mile further down the road Colette spontaneously pulls in by a small lake and to everyone's surprise she who's the sensible one, runs to the edge, takes off her shoes and strides in. 'It's freezing' she squeals, 'but lovely, come on in!' Suddenly sharing that urge to feel water on their feet and sand between their toes the others join her, splashing around with childlike satisfaction. As they meet each other's gaze, any self-consciousness at the novelty of the situation is outweighed by the pure joy of the moment. 'This is the perfect ending to our adventure,' announces Collette, and the others agree. Then they ease themselves back into the car and travel back to the hotel without further incident, each jealously savouring her own thoughts.

That evening at the hotel bar Jenny finds herself standing beside the lover and animatedly describes to him her role in the hunt. He congratulates her on finding the treasure. By this time of the evening he's in the maudlin stage of drunkenness and they have an earnest conversation about alcohol, he admitting that he has a problem with it and vowing to cut back. Jenny warmly encourages him in this, at the same time realising that in being witness to a resolution doomed to failure, she'll be someone to be avoided in future. Sure enough their tenuous bond is broken shortly afterwards by him getting up to order Diana and himself another drink.

Carol has always described this trip away each year as her therapy, her 'me' time away from the family. She'd painted a bright picture for Jenny of the fun they always had on these annual visits, the brilliant 'craic' the two groups experienced together. Observing everyone dispassionately Jenny wonders at this. Apart from Diana and the lover it seems to her that most interactions are pretty perfunctory, devoid of much nourishment. Carol continually tries to persuade one or other of the Galway people to re-tell a story that provided such entertainment back in the glory days but they never do. Maybe they had the performer's reluctance to try to recreate a masterpiece. Although Diana is adamant that the Galway group don't know of her affair Jenny suspects that in fact they do, and that as a consequence, the Belfast group are being held at arm's length. She's relieved that the next day they depart for home, saying their goodbyes for another year.

About eighteen months later when Diana had married her partner and moved with him to Spain, Jenny found herself in the unexpected position of being offered the opportunity to maybe fill her place, with the lover. It was after the Galway group had made a special visit to Belfast to perform in, what was for them, an uncharacteristically profound play. He took the lead role and she thought he was magnificent. Ironically, in playing someone else, he suddenly became more real to her as himself. Perhaps there was an element of conflating the man and the performance but he went from being a caricature to having heft, substance. They all had dinner afterwards and danced, and when the lights came up at the end of the evening he looked at her as though he'd never really seen her before, and told her that she was beautiful. 'It's the eyes,' he said, seemingly caught by them. Clichéd maybe, but she felt authenticity at its core. She also thought, wryly, that this was the ultimate compliment for a woman of her age – that she looked better in the bright than in the dark! They spent the rest of the evening in intimate conversation on the edge of the group, and she felt herself unfurl under his gaze, matching wit-to-wit and sparkling in a way that she feared was becoming increasingly rare for her.

But by then everything had become more problematic. For one thing, she'd met his wife. She was also more aware of the Galway group's general disapproval and of the surreptitious glances now cast her way. In spite of this she took pleasure in him escorting her back to her car, pleading like a small boy, for her to take him home with her. Hugging her he said, 'I'd be happy to just curl up in the back seat of your car all night if that's what you want!' Endearing as this was and though tempted, ultimately it was pride that held her back, a reluctance to be a substitute. She was also prosaic enough to spare an anxious thought about the chaotic state of the room she'd be taking him back to. So hoping that there'd be another, better, opportunity somewhere down the line she detached herself, got into the car and drove away, seeing him recede in the mirror, unmoving, staring as though by an act of will alone he could draw her back. Before she turned the corner she was already doubting her decision, recognising this chronic inability to seize the day as an eternal failing of hers.

The Galway group did perform in Belfast again the following year and Jenny went to see them, curious, open to possibility. However he had to rush away afterwards as his daughter had just arrived home from Canada, or so he said. Jenny suspected peer pressure. Other factors were involved including the death of a much-loved director, but after that the two groups seemed to mutually realise that their twenty-year relationship had come to a natural, or maybe an unnatural, end. They never performed together again.

The Belfast group lost its way a bit after that, members moving on to different projects. Jenny joined another drama group but occasionally meets up with Carol and Colette. Every year she receives a Christmas card from Diana in Spain, which reminds her of him; and then regrets for all lost opportunities crowd in her throat.

Thank you kindly

Last year I took the plunge and indulged in some sessions with a life coach in a belated attempt to find myself, or at least to unify some of the myriad of 'selfs' I chose to don each day according to mood or necessity. Gratitude was one of the topics we explored in the process. Now I'd never really thought much about gratitude before; well I knew that I gave it automatically where it was due, but this wasn't just about gratitude for services rendered but a weightier more fundamental gratitude, for life, nature, health and all the things I was already lucky enough to possess. And the aim was not just to have a passive appreciation of things, but to feel a real visceral thankfulness for them.

However this kind of gratitude requires a recipient. I recalled all those athletes in the last Olympics, who when they were interviewed after their event humbly attributed their victories to God, sketchily crossing themselves and flicking their gratitude upwards with a quick meaningful glance. The losers ... mmm, not so much! God was problematic for me – I'd begun to disown him many years back though I suspect he made the first move. However I am rather partial to a bit of quantum physics so I felt that I could usefully give my gratitude to some benevolent universal energy source.

When I thought of major reasons for feeling grateful in my past, I remembered those two long weeks in my early twenties when I feared I might be pregnant. God, who was still on the scene then, came up trumps. Huge relief, huge gratitude. Then for the time I managed to survive a bad accident, didn't fail in a challenging job, or to lesser events such as it not raining on a 'special' day. I recognised a theme here, most of my gratitude was for disasters avoided, for things that didn't happen rather than things that did. The few successes I'd had scattered here and there, winnowed from the chaff, I tended to attribute to my own good devices.

To practice gratitude I had to begin by listing each night ten things I'd been grateful for during the day, to read them aloud, and after each repeat 'thank you' three times. This nightly practice would be continued for a month. I was also advised to place a special 'gratitude stone' by my bedside and each night to hold it while contemplating the thing I was most grateful for that day. That bit was easy. I'd picked a stone from a deserted beach in Donegal, redolent of a wild Celtic energy that I hoped would somehow be potent enough to imbue me with gratitude.

The list of ten was more difficult. I started with the grand ones like being grateful for the sun, the moon, nature in all its forms, my house and car, progressing down to books, music, then down to maybe to getting a nice email from a friend, or my son making the dinner that night. I usually ran out of steam around number eight and was tempted to supplement the list with things of a more specious variety like being grateful for a half-friendly gesture from the cat when she wanted fed.

Still I persevered – with a little sleight of mind some things could, with validity, be repeated the next night with only minor variations. After a while I realised that it didn't really matter what I wrote, the process of writing itself made me more aware of all the good things I already had. And this acknowledgement improved my outlook, people responded to this accordingly which made me even more happy and grateful and so on... a self-perpetuating process, gaining momentum exponentially! When the month ended the practice was ingrained and I was able to reduce my ritual to three important things to celebrate each night.

But like any religion you have to put the hours in, and of course I frequently fell by the wayside. Like an alcoholic reneging on the 12-step programme I had to pick myself up and start again. Another motivation was the payback. Without giving it the full 'Uriah Heep' treatment, if you're nice to people they'll be nice back. It seems to me that Americans are instilled with this gratitude principle at birth along with their constitution, and millions of Americans can't be wrong, can they? Donald Trump. Say no more.

And then there's the amazing concept that you can be grateful for things you haven't yet received, and the very fact that you've put that gratitude out there makes it more likely to happen! Sticking with my quantum physics rationale, there's a principle that states that the very act of observing an atomic particle causes it to change its course. If they can do that then I've no problem in believing that those canny little critters can, energised by my strong feeling and when not observed, zip into the future and reassemble themselves into the object of my desire. Though that may owe more to Star Trek than to Einstein.

The one thing that I find hard to reconcile with the gratitude concept is that taken to its logical conclusion, does it not lead to global inertia? In an ideal world this should mean fewer wars but if everyone was grateful for just what they had would this not also prevent necessary revolutions or progress? Would there have been a women's movement? Would wives stay in abusive relationships grateful for each temporary lull? In this world, is it just more opium for the masses?

There's a divide in physics between the micro and the macro – few of us understand behaviour at particle level but we can all understand and accept it at macro level in the chairs and tables those particles form. In contrast I don't understand the gratitude concept at macro level so maybe I should just concentrate on the micro, my own small efforts, and living in the now.

Food for Thought

Sunday night teas in our house became a disappointment of epic proportions. Don't get me wrong, we weren't deprived, my mother always served up a hearty roast for lunch with all the trimmings. But those were the days of the first series of 'Masterchef' with Lloyd Grossman, and at 6pm each Sunday our family would be glued to the television listening to him describing, with his mid-Atlantic strangulated vowels, the taste of the likes of coq au vin and boeuf bourguignonne. Just when our salivation had reached its peak my mother would call us in for our tea and there on each plate would be the dreaded 'salad'.

Now this salad wasn't a lovely mixed concoction of artichokes, avocado, pomegranate seeds and lollo rosso tossed in a judicious blend of extra virgin olive oil and balsamic. No, this was a separatist salad with a large lettuce leaf, a tomato cut in half, three rounds of cucumber and the inevitable roll of processed ham artistically balanced on the side. It seemed that each ingredient eschewed touching each other – even the beetroot refrained from bleeding onto its neighbours, the only way to unite them being the application of a liberal dollop of salad cream.

Whatever happened to salad cream? I guess mayonnaise came on the scene, beating it hands down. Even the very name is superior. Mayonnaise trips off the tongue, a smorgasbord of elongated vowels whereas the early promise of the vowels in the words salad cream are let down by consonants bringing them to an abrupt end.

Apart from salads my mother's cooking was of the meat and two vegetables variety. I can't really recall having sauces of many kinds. I remember my sister's friend, who was a Protestant, describing how gravy featured highly in her family meals, even with Christmas dinner. Our family would have considered this a criminal act to perpetrate on our lovely dry spread, with its cranberry sauce carefully poised on the side. For years I thought that the main differences between Catholics and Protestants were the last line of the Lord's Prayer, and the fact that they had gravy and we didn't.

Is this when you realise that you've finally graduated from the family environment and made your own way in the world – when you reject the food of your childhood, almost view it with distain? When I left home I was drawn to stir fries and one pot cooking and though for years I've put this down to laziness and my ineptitude with a roast, I think I can now attribute it, with some credibility, to a rebellion against this separatist food of my childhood.

But I didn't reject it suddenly, it was a gradual process. In fact when I first went to live in London I had a boyfriend who was a chef, and I complained when he insisted on always using what I considered 'fancy' ingredients. For our Christmas dinner he would spend days boning and stuffing about five birds, from pigeon to goose, inside each other in incremental steps. The end result was a splendid though amorphous concoction. I didn't appreciate him at the time but could kick myself now when I recollect my eternal refrain of 'Please can we have something plain tonight!'

But years later I found myself in the position of having to give regular, informal dinner parties and not being a natural cook, looked for inspiration. Sainsbury's started producing a series of beautifully illustrated books of recipes from around the world and I snapped each one up as it was issued. I was adventurous, choosing dishes with ingredients that were an acquired taste, insisting that my guinea pigs acquire it pretty quickly. I revelled in the use of exotic herbs and spices and if I could ever claim to have a signature dish you'll find it amongst these well-thumbed little volumes, turmeric-stained pages still stuck together with the vestiges of former triumphs.

Eventually my son took over the cooking and when I had to produce the occasional meal, found myself resorting to the separatist food of my childhood. Salmon wrapped in foil in the oven, vegetables in the microwave, no sauces admitted, no pots or pans harmed in the process. Now he's moving away and unless he freezes a year's worth of meals for me in advance, I'll be left more permanently to my own devices. But this time I feel a growing urge to avoid regressing to banality; instead to rediscover all those old recipes and unglue the pages, to scour the backs of cupboards for all those spices optimistically purchased at various craft fairs, and to challenge myself once again. Friends may beware!

Gertrude's Lament – a monologue

I've always had a bad press ... 'Frailty thy name is woman,' and all that, but they don't know what it's like to have a son like Hamlet. Okay, so I helped murder his father and married his uncle, which doesn't exactly foster good family relations; but ladies and gentlemen, I was provoked! By the way the father issue has come back to haunt me, literally. Ghostly prowlings on the battlements by night, pouring poison about me into Hamlet's ear. Which is ironic considering that's how we despatched his father; you know, the poison ... in the ear ... thing. But that doesn't give Hamlet the right to behave like a petulant teenager.

I blame his friends; he got in with a bad crowd, like those celebrity wannabes Rosencrantz and Guildenstern. I wouldn't be surprised if they appeared in their own play one of these days. But hanging about in graveyards all the time – that can't be healthy. And the girlfriend, Ophelia, always floating around whimsically, posing in ponds for that Pre-Raphaelite Brotherhood. Bunch of radicals. Mark my words; she'll come to a bad end! He'd have been better off with one of those strong cross-dressing women like Portia or Rosamund – they'd have made a man of him.

I have to admit though – that speech of his was a stroke of genius. Much as I love him, let's face it, who would have remembered Hamlet without that catchphrase of his, 'To be or not to be?' Sheer self indulgence. If he were a real man, or indeed a woman, he'd have just got on with it. And he's always prattling on about nobility, but what was so noble about trying to flush out his uncle and me with a badly acted play – anyone could see where that one was going. Very sneaky. If anyone's suffering from 'outrageous fortune' it's me!

It's so frustrating to think he'll be the one to be remembered whereas I'll probably be written off as the dysfunctional mother. I wonder who'll play me in the movie – it would have to be a woman of a certain age, maybe Meryl Streep if she can master the accent, or Helen Mirren, she's good at queens isn't she? Hamlet would have to be played by someone … sensitive, shall we say, maybe even a woman.

Regrets? Of course I have regrets. I mean the Polonius incident was unfortunate, but think of it as collateral damage. Lurking around behind curtains is never a good idea. Being a queen isn't easy you know – Hamlet's dad never once asked for my opinion on anything. Don't get me wrong, I've never had a lust for power like my counterpart, that Macbeth woman. All I did was succumb to my smooth-talking brother-in-law whispering sweet nothings in my ear about equality. And Hamlet doesn't like me talking like this, but his dad really wasn't 'all that' in the bedroom department – at least his uncle Claudius knows how to treat a woman. Hamlet says I drive him mad. *He's* mad? How does he think I feel!

Oh dear, I don't think this is going to end well.

Imprinted

Ah Pygmalion, why so fainthearted?
You saw the Propoetides and their licentiousness dismayed
so you judged all women as depraved
punished them by creating your own Madonna
a statue in virginal ivory, me,
a tabula rasa on which to etch your desires
the manifestation of all your needs.
You preferred the shadow of the flesh
to the warm-blooded thing itself
and for a while my cold unresponsiveness soothed.
But you soon grew tired, wanted more
the actual embodiment of your labour
to create, like God, in your own image.
Your prayer was answered, I grew warm, breathed.

But Pygmalion, I could never really break free,
with each chiselled blow you'd curbed my spirit
just as surely as you'd carved my form.
How could I shape a separate life
already imbued with your desires
straight-jacketed by your expectations
limited to measured response
a parody, a cipher, the ideal trophy wife.
I'd never leave, but neither could I give you
the ultimate embrace.

If only you'd had the courage to trust,
we could have had a union of equals
matching breath-to-breath, flame-to-flame.
But instead you chose stale safeness.

Ah Pygmalion, you of little faith.

Less is More

Something plain,
no frills, pared down,
unadorned, unaffected, artless…
Not right, start again.
Just honest, concise.

A crowded room, across, eyes met,
no enchantment necessary.
She looked, he liked,
so far so good.
Possibilities shimmer electrically…
Not right, start again.

Smiles welcoming,
'You dancing?' I'm dancing'.
Fluent movements
spreading warmth.
A celestial choir harmonizes…
Not right, start again.

Sweet talk, restrained kiss,
union of bodies,
meeting of minds.
No stars aligning,
random chance.
That's better.

To be or not to be ... a muse

It is glorious to have the artist's worshipful beam
illuminate you, to luxuriate in that ultimate regard.
The gaze that acknowledges, bears witness to,
celebrates and immortalizes you and your beauty
in a way ordinary life denies.

But when that beam starts to wane
you're left in darkness, desolate,
somehow less than before,
something integral gone,
spirit leached out,
the taking of your image
simultaneously snaring
a piece of your soul.

You struggle to recover,
find a part of your core
to breathe life back into,
something to rebuild.

And there it is,
fitfully glowing
in the dark,
the small
ember of
your own
talent.